Brown Bread and Honey

by Pamela Allen

Adapted as a play by Mark Carthew

Illustrated by Pamela Allen

Series editor: Mark Carthew

D0486852

Collins

Characters

Narrator 1 (Storyteller)

Narrator 2 (Storyteller)

King

Stableboy

Maid

Gardener

Cooks (x6)

Minister for Money

Soldier

Turn to page **21** for Sound and Stage Tips

Brown Bread and Honey

Narrator 1:   The King was the most important person in the land. He lived in a big castle on top of a high hill.

Narrator 2:   With his friend the stableboy, he loved to jump, he loved to run and he loved to ride his horse.

(The King gallops around on a toy horse.)

Sound FX: *(Clip clop galloping noises.)*

Narrator 1:   But what he loved most of all was food.

Narrator 2: All day, every day, in the castle kitchen, the King's cooks cooked.

(The Cooks mime the actions.)

Cook 1: Stirring and whirring,
Mixing and fixing …

Cook 2: Basting and tasting,
Sniffing and whiffing …

Cook 3: Sipping and dipping,
Making and baking …

Cook 4: Chopping and lopping!

Cook 5: We stew and we brew …

Cook 6: Lots of yummy things for the King to chew.

All Cooks: We love cooking, yes we do!

Narrator 1: Until at last they had made the King's dinner. There were …

Cook 1: Milkshakes and muffins …

Cook 2: Puddings and pumpkins …

Cook 3: Chicken and chocolate …

Cook 4: Pavlova and pikelets …

Cook 5:   Curry and cordial …

Cook 6:   Custard pies and ice-cream cake.

All Cooks: As many yummy things
as we can make!

King: *(shouting)* Bring more food!
Bake! Bake! Bake!

Narrator 2:   The King managed to eat it all.

Narrator 1: But gradually, little by little, bit by bit, he got slower and slower and heavier and heavier.

Narrator 2: Until he was too slow to run, too tired to jump and too heavy for his poor horse. Nothing he did was fun any more.

Narrator 1: The King was miserable. Nothing he ate tasted good any more. As each splendid new dish reached the table, the King complained.

(The Cooks offer the King their meals. He screws up his face and complains each time.)

King: This curry is too hot!
This gravy is too greasy!
These muffins are too mushy!
This stuffing is too sticky!

(The Cooks walk sadly offstage.)

Narrator 2: The cooks were sad and they tried harder and harder to make bigger and better dishes to please the King.

(The Cooks re-enter and place plates of new meals before the King.)

Narrator 1: Then one evening, after a big dinner of pork pie, pease pudding and pavlova, the King was sick.
VERY SICK.

King: *(groaning)*

OOOOOH! AAAAAH!

OOOOOOH!

11

Narrator 2: Now he was SO miserable and SO tired that he didn't want to see another pie, pudding or pavlova ever again.

King: *(To the Cooks.)* It's all your fault! You're sacked!

(The Cooks pack their bags and leave, looking sad.)

Narrator 1: Now there were no cooks left in the castle.

Narrator 2: The next morning the King felt a little better and wanted some breakfast. He asked the maid who cleaned the kitchen …

King: Can you cook?

Narrator 1: But the maid had heard him complaining about the curry and she remembered what had happened to the cooks.

Maid: *(Shaking her head.)* No, I can't.

Narrator 2: Then he asked the gardener
who grew the gardenias.

King: Can you cook?

Narrator 1: But the gardener had heard him
grizzling about the gravy.

Gardener: *(Shaking his head.)* No, I can't.

Narrator 2: Then he asked the minister in charge of the money.

King: Can you cook?

Narrator 1: But the minister had heard him moaning about the muffins.

Minister for Money: *(Shaking his head.)* No, I can't.

Narrator 2: Then he asked the soldier who served as the sentry.

King: Can you cook?

Narrator 1: But the soldier had heard him screeching about the stuffing.

Soldier: *(Shaking his head.)* No, I can't.

Narrator 2: When there was no one left to ask, the King sat down just where he was and cried.

King: *(sobbing)* Boo, hoo! Boo, hoo!

Narrator 1: He was still sitting there the next day when the stableboy found him.

(The Stableboy holds out the lunch his mother had made and offers it to the King.)

Stableboy: Would you like some brown bread and honey, Your Majesty?

Narrator 2: Now the King had never tasted brown bread in his life. He stopped crying. He looked at it carefully.

(The King sniffs the bread.)

BUT HE DIDN'T COMPLAIN.

King: Thank you. *(He takes a bite.)* This is yummy!

Narrator 1: The King greedily gobbled up ALL of the stableboy's lunch and was looking around for more.

King: Do you have any more sandwiches?

Stableboy: There isn't any more. That's all there is.

King: I'm sorry. But I was SO-O-O hungry.

Narrator 2: Each day from then on, the stableboy brought two lunches in two little boxes to the castle—one for the King and one for himself—and together they would sit under a shady tree to eat.

(They sit down and eat the sandwiches.)

Narrator 1: Until ... at last ... the King could jump and run and ride his horse again.

(The King gallops around on a toy horse.)

Sound FX: *(Clip clop galloping noises.)*

Narrator 2: This made the King very happy.

Cook 1: Now he loves messing about in the castle kitchen, making meals with his friend the stableboy.

Cook 2: And do you know what they like best of all?

All: BROWN BREAD AND HONEY!

Sound and Stage Tips

About This Play

This play is a story you can read with your friends in a group or act out in front of an audience. Before you start reading, choose a part or parts you would like to read or act. There are fourteen speaking parts in this play, including the Narrators and Cooks, so make sure you have readers for all the parts. The Cooks could be played by a small group of six, or you could have three Cooks doubling up, or as many as you like!

Reading the Play

It's a good idea to read the play through to yourself before you read it as part of a group. It is best to have your own book, as that will help you too. As you read the play through, think about each character and how they might look and sound. How are they behaving? What sort of voice might they have?

Rehearsing the Play

Rehearse the play a few times before you perform it for others. In *Brown Bread and Honey*, the Cooks have fun making their meals. Practise offering the King all the different yummy meals. If you rehearse the play beforehand, you can decide where each of the players can best stand and move, and how each one can react to the King's bad manners.

Remember you are an actor as well as a reader. Your facial expressions and the way you move your body will really help the play to come alive!

Using Your Voice

Remember to speak out clearly and be careful not to read too quickly! Speak more slowly than you do when you're speaking to your friends. Keep in mind that the audience is hearing your words for the first time.

The rhyming descriptions of cooking in this play are very funny, so make sure the audience can understand the words and meaning of each phrase. Practise saying aloud the rhyming words, such as sniffing and whiffing! You should also practise saying the King's 'Ooohs!' and 'Aaahs!' when he feels sick.

From time to time, look at the audience as well as the other actors. Be sure that everyone can hear what you are saying.

Creating Sound Effects (FX)

Adding sound effects (FX) throughout the play can provide extra atmosphere. You could make up sounds to match the cooking actions, such as stirring and whirring, and also the sound of the horse galloping. See if there are other parts in this play where you could add sound effects.

Sets and Props

Once you have read the play, make a list of the things you will need.
Here are some ideas to help your performance. You may like to add
some of your own.

- Cooking bowls
- Large stirring spoons
- Trays and plates
- Food, fake or real!
- King's table and chair
- Six bags for the Cooks
- Cloth and bucket for the Maid
- Rake or spade for the Gardener
- Money bags for the Minister for Money
- Two lunch boxes
- Brown bread sandwiches
- Toy horse

Costumes

This play can be performed with or without costumes. If you wish to
dress up, you may find the following useful.

- Crown and robe for the King
- Chefs' hats for the Cooks
- Simple costume for the Stableboy,
  such as jeans, checked shirt and a hat
- Uniform for the Soldier
- Apron for the Maid
- Jacket and tie for the Minister for Money
- Overalls for the Gardener

Have fun!

Ideas for reading

Written by Kelley Taylor
Educational Consultant

Learning objectives: be aware of different voices in stories using dramatised readings, showing differences between the narrator and different characters used; read, prepare and present playscripts; take account of the grammar and punctuation when reading aloud; collect new words from reading and categorise them, e.g. verbs, nouns, adjectives; comment constructively on plays and performance, discussing effects and how they are achieved

Curriculum links: Science: Health and growth; Citizenship: Children's rights – human rights

Interest words: stableboy, galloping, miserable, pavlova, complaining, gardenias, sentry

Resources: whiteboards or paper, musical instruments, paper and cardboard

Casting: (1) Narrator 1 & Cook 1 (2) Narrator 2 & Cook 2 (3) King & Cook 3 (4) Stableboy and Cook 4 (5) Maid and Cook 5 (6) Involve the whole group in sound FX

Getting started

- Explain to the group that this play has a message. Ask the children to predict what this message could be, focusing particularly on the pictures on pp6–11.

- Read the list of characters on p2. Ensure that the children understand the meaning and importance of the narrator. Explore a range of voices that could be used to read each part.

- Highlight the interesting verbs and nouns that relate to food. Discuss how words can be broken up into their root words, e.g. *mix – ing*, or into chunks, e.g. *pav – lo – va*, to make them easier to decode.

Reading and responding

- Ask the children to read pp3–9 silently, reflecting on the personalities of the characters. Ask them to suggest the kinds of voices they could use.

- Look at pp4–5. How is each line affected by the ellipses? How could the verbs (e.g. *basting* and *tasting*) be read for added impact?

- Ask the children to read pp10–17 silently and reflect on the role of the narrators. Can the children explain why a narrator is used? (e.g. to hold the story together)

- Ask the group to discuss how they feel about the King. Are they sympathetic? Why/why not? What should happen next? Read to the end, and then discuss the message of the story.